Happy Birthday, Eeyore!

Disney's
Winnie the Pooh First Readers

Disney's

A Winnie the Pooh First Reader

Happy Birthday, Eeyore!

Isabel Gaines
Illustrated by Studio Orlando

Random House 🏠 New York

Printed in the United States of America

Library of Congress number: 00-108680
ISBN: 0-7364-1139-9 (paperback)

First Random House Edition: January 2001

www.randomhouse.com/kids/disney
www.disneybooks.com

Happy Birthday, Eeyore!

Eeyore was in his sad spot
when Pooh stopped by.

"Eeyore, why are you
so sad?" Pooh asked.
"It's my birthday," said Eeyore.

7

"Your birthday?" asked Pooh.

"Of course," said Eeyore.

"Can't you see the presents?"

Pooh looked around.

"No," said Pooh.

"The cake and candles?"

asked Eeyore.

"Well, no," said Pooh.

"Neither can I," Eeyore said sadly.

That gave Pooh an idea.

He said, "Eeyore,

wait right here."

Pooh ran to his house.

Piglet was there

looking for him.

"I must get

poor Eeyore a present,"

Pooh said. "But what?"

Pooh looked

around his house.

He saw a small
honeypot
on his shelf.
"Of course!
Honey!"
cried Pooh.
"Piglet, what are you
giving Eeyore?"
"Well, I could give him
my red balloon,"
Piglet said.

"Good idea," Pooh said.
Piglet went home
to find the balloon.
Pooh left to give
Eeyore his present.

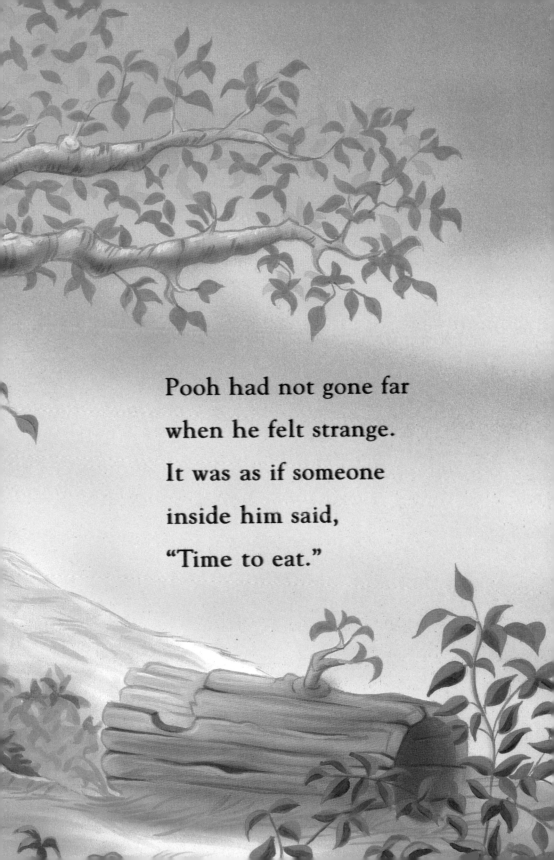

Pooh had not gone far
when he felt strange.
It was as if someone
inside him said,
"Time to eat."

Pooh sat down
and ate the honey
in the honeypot.
He ate and ate.

When he had licked
the last sticky drop,
Pooh asked, "Now, where was
I going?

"Oh yes—to Eeyore's.
Oh bother! Now what
will I give Eeyore?"
Pooh began to think.

"I know!" said Pooh.

"A honeypot without honey

is a *useful* pot.

Eeyore can put whatever

he wants in it."

At the same time, Piglet carried
a red balloon to Eeyore.
"Hello, Piglet!" he heard
from above.

Piglet looked up.

Owl was flying over him.

Piglet did not see

the tree in his path.

POP! Piglet crashed
into the tree.
"Oh d-d-d-dear," said Piglet.
"The balloon broke."

25

Piglet arrived
at Eeyore's house.
"Eeyore, here is
a birthday present
for you."

Piglet handed
the broken red balloon
to Eeyore.

Eeyore sadly looked
at the shredded red balloon.
Then Pooh arrived.

"I've brought you
a present, Eeyore," Pooh said.
"It's a useful pot."

29

Eeyore picked up the balloon
and dropped it in the pot.

"Eeyore, I am glad I gave you
that pot," said Pooh.
"And I am glad
that I gave you something
to put into the pot,"
added Piglet.

31

Just then, Christopher Robin
and Eeyore's other friends
arrived.

Christopher Robin led them all
to Rabbit's house.

They had a birthday party for Eeyore.

Eeyore did not say much.

But he looked very, very happy.